THE WINTER WISH

For my parents
H. M.

To my family, for giving me many years of
creative and memorable Christmases
R. D.

First published in hardback in the United Kingdom by HarperCollins*Publishers* Ltd in 2022

HarperCollins *Children's Books* is a division of HarperCollins*Publishers* Ltd
1 London Bridge Street, London SE1 9GF

www.harpercollins.co.uk

HarperCollins*Publishers*
1st Floor, Watermarque Building, Ringsend Road, Dublin 4, Ireland

1 3 5 7 9 10 8 6 4 2

Text copyright © Helen Mortimer 2022
Illustrations copyright © Rachael Dean 2022

ISBN: 978-0-00-849756-9

Printed and bound in Italy by rotolito S.p.A

THE WINTER WISH

WRITTEN BY HELEN MORTIMER

ILLUSTRATED BY RACHAEL DEAN

HarperCollins *Children's Books*

Ever since he was a baby, William
lived with Mum, Dad and Rufford
in a tiny flat above their shop.

Now he was six years old and thirty-seven books tall.
And there were only eleven days till Christmas.

WORDS OF WONDER was cosy, warm and piled
high with books. And William loved it.

There were books that took you to faraway places, books
that were filled with delicious dishes and beautiful
picture books with jewel-bright pages.

There were squashy sofas where you could share a story with Rufford, and there were jars of Dad's homemade gingerbread on the counter for customers who came in to browse . . .

The trouble was, there weren't many customers.

You see WORDS OF WONDER was at the far
end of a street right on the edge of town.

TEXTILES

BETTY'S

It was the kind of town where everyone hurried,
heads down, to get home on cold winter days.

"I'm not sure how much longer we can keep our
little shop going," sighed Mum one evening.
"We might have to close by Christmas."

Her words hit William like a cold snowball.
He couldn't let it happen.
He had to save the shop.

In the morning William slipped out with Rufford before breakfast and came back with armfuls of dry leaves and twigs.

He raided the recycling box.

He worked hard all day, cutting, painting and sticking, until . . .

William was ready.

He led Mum and Dad outside, saying, "Keep your eyes closed until I say you can open them!"

In William's winter window, a leafy reindeer with twig antlers
pulled a painted cardboard sleigh filled with mossy cushions and
stacked with books. Shiny stars sparkled all around, and a foil
bell hung from the reindeer's neck.

"It's wonderful!" said Dad. William's winter window
glowed brightly. But the street was dark and empty.
William wasn't sure if his window would be enough.

That night, William was woken by a tinkling sound.

Arrrf? Rufford let out a little question-bark.
"Come on," said William. "Let's investigate."

The shop was full of shadows. Only the window was lit up.
And that's when William saw . . .

GINGER

OPEN

. . . the reindeer lift its head and smile.

"Hello," she said. "I'm Bracken."
"You're real!" whispered William.
"Sometimes," said Bracken, "but only in places
where there's a special kind of magic."

William and Rufford climbed into the sleigh.
"Does that mean *you* are magic?" asked William.

The answer came in a sudden lurch from the sleigh and a rush of icy air against William's face. They were flying.

William and Rufford cuddled close as Bracken whooshed them over rooftops and towards the fields and woods beyond.

"Can your magic do anything?" he said. "Can it save our shop?"

"Your winter window was where the magic started," said Bracken.

"Together we'll find a way."

When they stopped for a rest, William found some
fresh ferns for Bracken and stroked her soft nose.
His head was full of questions.

As they flew back over the town, stars sparkled above them.
Bracken looked down at the dark streets below. It gave her an idea.

"Words can be magic . . ." she said. "Let's call out all the shiniest words we know!"
"*Twinkle!*" shouted William . . . and a window suddenly burst into colour and light.

"*Glitter!*" "*Shimmer!*"   "*Glow!*"   "*Dazzle!*"

When their magical journey was
over, William gave Bracken a hug.
"Goodnight," he said. "And thank you."

The town was still sleeping as William and Rufford tiptoed back to bed and Bracken settled once more – quiet, leafy and unstirring – in the window.

In the morning William heard some very strange
sounds. Outside, there was chatter and laughter.
People were not hurrying – they were lingering
and looking. Their faces were as bright as the
windows that lined William's street.

All through the day families squeezed into WORDS of WONDER.
"We've never been so busy!" said Mum.
"It's all thanks to your winter window," said Dad.

Christmas Eve came and the little
bookshop was still bustling.

When it was time to close for the holidays
Mum, Dad and William breathed a sigh of
happiness. Now they could look forward
to warm, festive days off.

That night, William was woken – once again – by a tinkling sound. But this time, it was different. At first it was a distant ringing from the sky above. Then Bracken's bell joined in from the shop below them.

William knew at once what it meant. He crept to his window with
Rufford just in time to see Bracken flying past . . . to join Santa's sleigh.
"Goodbye, Bracken," William murmured.

And with Mum, Dad and Rufford on Christmas morning, William knew he was surrounded by a special kind of magic.